THE ELECTRONIC OLYMPICS

THE ELECTRONIC OLYMPICS

by Hal Higdon

HOLT, RINEHART AND WINSTON
New York   Chicago   San Francisco

BOOKS BY HAL HIGDON

The Electronic Olympics
The Horse That Played Center Field

FOR THE MUSACCHIOS

CHAPTER 1 David Henderson ran swiftly through the long airport corridor. He dodged around two men with suitcases. He slowed to avoid hitting a woman carrying a baby. "Which way is gate two?" he asked a man in a blue uniform.

The man pointed to the right. Dave shifted his camera case to another shoulder then started running again.

Several hundred people stood jammed around gate two. Many carried posters. WELCOME HOME CHAMP, read one. NEXT STOP OLYMPICS, read another. The crowd included TV cameramen and newspaper reporters.

Dave spotted a reporter he knew. "Has Speed's plane arrived yet?"

The reporter shook his head.

Dave sighed in relief and set his case down. All that running for nothing. He removed two cameras from the case and put them around his neck. Next he aimed a light meter toward the entrance gate. Quickly he adjusted the camera lenses. An airplane taxied toward them. "Here he comes!" someone shouted.

The crowd hushed. They had come to greet their local hero: miler Speed Sloan. Two days earlier the young athlete had outrun America's best runners at 1500 meters. Speed finished first at the Olympic trials. He thus earned a place on the United States team that would compete in the Olympic Games that summer. The games would take place for the first time in the small country of Scandia.

Dave Henderson worked as a photographer for *Sports Weekly*. The magazine wanted a feature story on Speed Sloan. "Follow him around for a week," the photo editor had told Dave. "Shoot everything he does. He might be the next Olympic champion."

The airport crowd suddenly roared. Speed Sloan appeared in the gateway. The tall athlete raised his arms over his head in a victory salute.

Dave squinted through his view finder. He focused on Speed. *Click.* Dave shot one picture then thumbed a lever on top of the camera to advance the film. *Click. Click.*

In a matter of seconds Dave snapped a dozen pictures of Speed Sloan waving to the crowd. Then he moved several steps to his right and framed another shot. *Click. Click. Click.*

"We want Speed!" chanted the crowd. "We want Speed!"

Dave switched to the second camera. It had a wide-angle lens. Looking through the view finder he could see the entire crowd. Speed stood in the middle. Next to him was Dr. Ken Costello, a computer scientist. Dr. Costello directed the sports lab where Speed Sloan trained.

A TV announcer shoved a microphone at the runner. "How do you think you'll do at the Olympic Games, Speed?"

"I'll win the gold medal," Speed answered almost automatically.

Dave grimaced. He had photographed Speed before. In his two years with *Sports Weekly*, Dave Henderson had never met an athlete with more talent—or more conceit. Well, maybe it wasn't Speed's fault. He always won. He never knew what it was like to lose.

"You expect to win?" prodded a reporter.

"As long as they don't allow four-legged people in the race," replied the runner. He flashed a grin. Everybody laughed.

Oh brother, thought Dave. Listen to Bob Hope. What a jerk. Yet the sports writers had built Speed Sloan into the great all-American hero. He looked clean cut. Big smile. The public didn't know that after he stopped running, Speed Sloan turned into a louse.

But Dave didn't permit his private views to get in the way of his job. He climbed on top of a chair to get a shot of the crowd. Meanwhile, a large, bald-headed man pushed his way through the crowd to stand near Speed. Dave saw it was millionaire Peter Powell. He owned a large electronics company that built computers. He also served as president of the Olympic committee. Powell had one arm thrust around Speed's shoulders. He always managed to get his face in photographs.

"Ladies and gentlemen," Powell shouted. "As long as we continue to produce boys like Speed Sloan, America will always be great!" The crowd erupted in cheers. Powell grinned for the TV cameras.

That'll be good for business, thought Dave, shaking his head in disgust. Then, switching cameras again, he focused for a close-up. A slender girl with short dark hair appeared in his view finder. Dave knew her from somewhere. She handed Speed a bouquet of flowers. Speed bent down and kissed her on the cheek.

"Who's the girl?" Dave asked a young man standing nearby.

"Stacy Randolph," came the answer.

"Is that Speed's girl friend?"

The youth squinted up at him. "You want to get hit?"

Dave climbed down off the chair to load more film into his camera. "That must be your girl then," he said.

The youth shook his head. "No, she's my cousin. I just think she can do better than Speed Sloan."

Stacy Randolph. Dave suddenly recalled why he knew the girl. She was a platform diver. Dave had covered the Olympic trials in diving two weeks earlier. Stacy Randolph was the girl who used a metal frog for a good luck charm. She would place it near the edge of the pool before she dove. It seemed to work —Stacy had made the American team. She looked cute. Dave decided he would like to know Stacy Randolph better.

The speeches ended and the crowd started to leave. Peter Powell and Dr. Costello climbed into a long Cadillac and drove away. Speed walked with Stacy.

Dave decided to say hello. "Remember me, Speed?" Dave said offering his hand. "Dave Henderson from *Sports Weekly*. I'll be trailing you this week taking pictures."

"Sure, I remember you, Henderson," said the runner. He turned toward Stacy and said, "This guy is almost as fast with his cameras as I am with my spikes." Stacy smiled sweetly. Dave winced.

"Pleased to meet you, Dave," said the girl.

"Hi," responded Dave, then couldn't think of anything more to say.

Speed Sloan meanwhile had noticed the youth standing next to Dave. "Here, Rabbit. Go run over and pick up my bags." Speed handed him a baggage check.

The youth accepted the check. "Sure, Speed."

He turned to go, but tripped over a box of TV gear. The boy called Rabbit almost fell, but caught himself and ran off to the baggage counter. Speed Sloan let loose a roar of laughter.

"Speed, that wasn't funny," said Stacy.

"Rabbit doesn't mind," answered the runner.

"Rabbit?" asked Dave. "Is that his real name?"

"Well, most people call him Larry—Larry Spitzig," said Speed. "But I call him Rabbit because he leads the early laps in some of my races. You know— sets pace like a mechanical rabbit." Speed laughed once more.

You're a sweet kid, Speed, thought Dave. But I guess I'm stuck with you—at least for a week.

CHAPTER 2 The next day, Speed Sloan ran nearly two hours without moving more than a few inches. The miler worked out in a laboratory on a treadmill, a rubber belt that moved beneath him. The treadmill's engine hummed smoothly. Speed's flat-bottomed shoes hit *pit-pat-pit-pat* on the moving belt. The only other sound in the room was the clicking of Dave Henderson's camera. Larry Spitzig sat on a bench beside the wall, looking bored.

"Sixty seconds, Speed," announced Dr. Costello. He pushed a button making the belt move faster. Speed shifted his pace.

The runner breathed into a long tube that measured his breath. He had wires taped to his chest. They connected to an electric device. A paper tape rolled from it showing Speed's heartbeat. A dial on another machine gave his temperature.

Dave stood before the treadmill. His camera pointed at the runner. "Ten seconds," said Dr. Costello. The belt moved still faster. Speed sprinted to keep up with it. Dave snapped a picture.

Then a buzzer sounded and the belt ground to a halt. Speed leaned against the handrails. Though breathing hard, he looked as though he could have run for another hour.

Dr. Costello pressed a stethoscope against the runner's chest. The doctor smiled then moved to look at the tapes from the machine. Dave peered over the doctor's shoulder. Larry peered over Dave's shoulder. "Does it give the score for last night's ball game?" Larry asked. The scientist pretended not to hear.

Dr. Costello moved to a teletype machine connected by phone line to a computer in Peter Powell's headquarters many miles away. He tapped the keyboard, feeding in the data just collected. Within seconds a viewing scope on the machine flashed back a series of numbers. Dr. Costello nodded. Finally he said to Speed Sloan, "According to my figures, you can break the world record."

Speed Sloan smiled, as though he already knew it.

"This weekend if you want to," added the scientist.

"I'll save my record for the Olympics," said Speed. "No sense wasting it on only a few thousand people."

The doctor nodded as though he agreed. "Will four minutes for the mile be fast enough for the track meet this weekend?"

Speed said it would.

Dr. Costello turned back to the computer keyboard. He punched SLOAN 4:00, and then GO. The teletype chattered like a machine gun. When it finished Dr. Costello tore off a sheet filled with numbers and handed them to Speed. "Here's your workout plan for the rest of the week," said the scientist. "Also the pace at each 110-yard mark for Saturday's mile. Now go shower."

Speed picked up a towel and started to go. He paused at the door. "Why don't you ask Rabbit to run on your treadmill, Doc," he said. "Just hang a carrot in front of his nose."

"Ha ha," said Larry after Speed had left. "Very funny."

"Did you ever run on the treadmill?" Dave asked him.

"Yes, but I kept falling off," admitted Larry. "I couldn't get used to the even pace. Besides, it made me feel like a squirrel in a cage." He left to follow Speed.

"If you saw Larry's test results," said Dr. Costello after the runner had gone, "you'd wonder how he runs even as fast as he does. He has no talent. His only asset is desire. On the other hand, Speed is a running machine."

"Is he as good as you say?" asked Dave. He had begun to pack his cameras into his case.

"I've seen data on most of the runners he will face in the Olympics," replied the doctor. "They don't stand a chance against him."

"What if the running machine breaks down?"

"It won't happen," said the doctor. "We watch him too closely. We test him each week. Every move he makes in training is computed in advance. His meals are preplanned. He goes to sleep when told. He gets up on schedule. Nothing can go wrong."

"Doesn't that take the sport out of it?" asked Dave.

The doctor shrugged. "I don't decide that. I only program the computer."

Dr. Costello walked over to a filing cabinet and removed a folder marked with Speed's name. He spread the contents on a desk. The papers described Speed Sloan's workouts. On one day Speed had run twenty 110-yard sprints in the morning. In the afternoon he had taken a series of five-minute runs on the treadmill. There was data on the amount of rest between each run, including his pulse rate. Nothing seemed left to chance.

Dave quickly figured that Speed, running twice a day, averaged 120 to 150 miles a week. "But shouldn't track be a sport and not a business?" suggested Dave once more.

The doctor shrugged. "It's the price one pays for greatness. An Olympic gold medal is worth any effort. To win one today, an athlete must be perfect."

Dave glanced again at the charts and graphs on the doctor's desk. With relief he noted that tomorrow Speed would be running outdoors on the track. At least he could get away from the air-conditioned dullness of Dr. Costello's laboratory.

Dave slung his camera case over his shoulder. "It's good to know," he mumbled as he pushed open the door to leave, "that something in this world can be perfect."

CHAPTER 3

Speed Sloan ran with the effortless grace of a deer. His feet seemed barely to graze the hard surface of the track. His arms swung in perfect rhythm with his legs.

Behind him ran Larry Spitzig. Larry struggled to match Speed's pace. Speed had been running on the track nearly an hour, doing "interval" training. First a fast lap, then a slow lap, then another fast lap. Sprint—jog—sprint—jog. On and on and on. He timed himself by watching a large clock on a pole beside the track. Every fourth lap Speed halted long enough to check his pulse. Then on and on and on.

While Speed and Larry ran, Dave Henderson shot pictures. He photographed Speed from all sides. He used every lens in his camera case from wide-angle to telephoto. Dave somehow doubted that the pictures would be much good. There was a certain sameness about everything Speed Sloan did.

Speed sprinted past again, but Larry slowed. The young runner jogged to where Dave had his camera gear and sat down gasping for breath. "He's inhuman," Larry told Dave, "like that bird in the Roadrunner cartoons."

Speed circled the track once more. "Beep, beep," said Larry, then he lay back on the grass and groaned.

"Why continue to run with him?" asked Dave.

Larry thought a moment. "I always wanted to run in the big track meets, only I wasn't fast enough. One day a meet promoter needed someone to set a fast pace for Speed on the first lap, then get out of the way. So I became a rabbit.

"Now I run in the big meets. I lead at the start. That assures the crowd of a fast time. Speed wins and I struggle home last. At first it was fun, but not any more."

"Believe me," said Dave. "It's not much fun taking pictures of him either."

"Who would you rather photograph?"

Dave grinned. "How about your cousin, Stacy? Of course, she's Speed's girl friend."

"Aw, Stacy doesn't like Speed that much," said Larry. "The only thing they have in common is the Olympic team."

13

Speed came past them one more time. Dave focused his camera on the passing runner. He pushed the button. It fired *click-click-click-click-click*.

Larry raised himself on his elbows. "You sure have enough cameras. That one fires like a machine gun."

"It's called a remote control camera," explained Dave. "It works automatically like a robot."

"Just like Speed," Larry grumbled.

"It's great for covering sports," Dave continued. "You just press the button and it shoots three frames a second, almost like a movie camera. That way you don't miss any action."

Larry no longer seemed tired. "What other tricks do you have?"

"I don't know if they're tricks," said the photographer. "I have a radio control unit that goes with the camera. Say I want to take pictures of a race from both sides of the track. I can place one camera on a tripod a hundred yards away. By using my radio unit I can shoot the camera by electric signal."

Speed appeared once more jogging easily. As he moved past the clock, he began another fast lap. On and on and on.

Dave watched him for a few moments, then reached for his camera case. "Let me show you something else." He rummaged through the case until he found a pair of shoes. They looked like regular track shoes, but when Dave turned them over Larry saw the shoes had roller bearings instead of spikes.

14

"What are those?"

"Roller shoes," Dave answered. "They're custom made. I figured I could skate beside the runners and take pictures during a race. You can do that now with the new hard-surface tracks. I tried them in a track meet last April."

"What happened?"

"Two things," said Dave. "First, I got going so fast I slid off the turn into the water pit. Second, five angry officials kicked me out of the stadium."

"Nice try," said Larry.

Speed passed by once more on a fast lap. Crossing the finish line he paused with one hand over his heart to check his pulse rate. Then he started to jog again.

A man carrying a suitcase approached. He addressed Larry. "How soon before Sloan is finished?"

"Maybe a half hour," Larry replied.

"Tell him I'll be over in the dressing room," the man said.

After the man left, Dave asked: "Who's he?"

"He works for one of the sports companies," explained Larry. "They make Simba shoes. They're gold colored. He wants Speed to run wearing the Simba brand."

Dave turned to look at the man walking away. At the Olympic Games in Mexico City a scandal had erupted over track shoes. Two companies had competed for name athletes. They wanted to advertise that their shoes had won many Olympic victories. There had been payoffs. Several athletes had been caught accepting money. This violated the amateur rules of the Olympics.

"Does he pay runners to wear his shoes?" Dave asked.

"He never offered me any money," laughed Larry.

"And I suppose you'll never get Speed Sloan to admit anything," added Dave.

Larry picked up the pair of roller shoes. "Now if somebody wanted a fast shoe," he said, "he ought to try these."

On the track Speed Sloan finally had stopped his interval running. He began putting on his sweat clothes. The runner would spend nearly twenty more minutes jogging on the grass cooling down. Dave grabbed a camera and moved toward him.

Larry remained seated. He still held the roller shoes in his hand. Suddenly he laughed. "Hey Dave," he called. "Do you think a rabbit on roller skates could beat a running machine?"

Dave was thirty yards away adjusting his camera for another picture of Speed. "What?" he shouted, looking back over his shoulder.

"Nothing," said Larry. "Nothing. I just got a funny idea." Then he rose and joined Speed in his cool-down jog.

16

CHAPTER 4

Stacy Randolph paused near the edge of the diving platform. For a moment she stood still, her slender figure outlined against the blue sky. Then she took two steps and a hop. Once, twice, three times she somersaulted in mid air.

Dave Henderson had just come from the nearby track. Speed and Larry had finished their workout and now were taking showers. Dave watched as the girl sliced into the blue waters of the pool. She caused hardly a splash.

Stacy pulled herself out of the pool and reached

for a towel. She wore a red, white, and blue tank suit. She jiggled when she walked. They'll never replace *that* with a computer, Dave thought.

The girl climbed the stairs back to the platform. Dave reached inside his case for a camera. As Stacy stood on top he focused on her. Stacy dove and Dave snapped a picture of her unwinding from her third somersault.

Stacy toweled herself and walked over to where Dave stood. "Hi," said the girl. "Does this mean I'll make the cover of *Sports Weekly*?"

Dave lowered the camera. "I'm off duty," he explained. "I took the picture for myself. I wanted a photograph of the famous girl with the frog." Dave pointed at the frog perched at the edge of the pool beneath the diving platform.

"Oh that," said Stacy. "Good luck charm." She walked over to retrieve it.

The girl diver held the frog in one hand. It was made of stainless steel. Dave recalled that the frog once had belonged to a girl who swam the 100-meter free style. She never lost a race. She retired with an Olympic gold medal, then gave the frog to Stacy. Maybe it could bring good luck.

"Speed Sloan runs by computer and Stacy Randolph dives with a frog," said Dave.

"I guess we all need help," laughed Stacy. "I could do without my frog, easier than Speed could do without his computer."

"You could do without Speed too," said a voice

behind them. Larry had arrived after dressing. "Hey cousin, I hear you're dating America's fastest miler after the track meet on Saturday."

Stacy frowned. "How do you know? Did Speed tell you?"

"No, it's posted in the locker room. You're programmed into his training schedule this week."

"You're a riot," said the girl. "Besides, what business is it of yours if I date him now and then? I date a lot of other guys too."

Larry continued, "By the way, Dr. Costello wants you to stop by the laboratory for some tests. You know—heartbeat, blood count. Nothing left to chance with Speed Sloan."

The girl raised the frog as though ready to throw it. "You want to get hit with a frog?" she said. "Besides, you're jealous because he runs faster than you."

"I am not!"

"Jealous rabbit! Jealous rabbit!" sang the girl. She stuck her tongue out at Larry.

"Maybe Stacy's right," said Dave. "If you had a chance to win at the Olympics, you might hop on that treadmill every morning too."

Larry shook his head. "No, never. I'd never become a machine like him." He paused. "Besides, I may have found a way to beat Speed this weekend."

"Jealous rabbit! Jealous rabbit!" continued the girl diver.

"Be quiet, Stacy," said Larry frowning. "If you weren't my cousin, I'd take that frog of yours and serve it for dinner. Stainless steel frog legs. Dr. Costello's computer says I need more iron in my diet."

The three of them laughed. Suddenly Larry snapped his fingers. "I almost forgot," he said. "Dave, you just had a phone call from your magazine. Something about taking pictures of Peter Powell tomorrow."

The Olympic chief, Dave thought. Well, he could use a day away from Speed Sloan, his stopwatch, and his treadmill.

CHAPTER 5 The escalator slid gracefully upward to the offices of Powell Electronic Devices. David Henderson rose with it, camera case slung over his shoulder. When he had called his photo editor the night before, Dave had been ordered to attend a two o'clock press conference. Olympic chief Peter Powell would preside.

"Do you have any idea what Powell wants?" Dave asked another newsman on the escalator.

"Probably got some new device up his sleeve," said the other man.

21

A clock above the escalator flashed the time to the nearest second: 1:59:23 . . . 1:59:24 . . . 1:59:-25 . . . .

"Looks like we're exactly on time," Dave remarked.

A voice suddenly crackled from a loudspeaker set in the ceiling. "You have thirty seconds before the press conference begins."

"It's almost as though it heard me," mumbled Dave.

At the end of the hallway, two broad doors beckoned. They bore the five-ring Olympic symbol. Dave raised his hand to push the doors open. Instantly, they slid noiselessly aside to reveal a room full of reporters.

"Magic," commented Dave.

"No," said the newsman. "Just Peter Powell. Everything he touches turns to electronic tape."

Three sides of the room were bare. A curtain covered the fourth side. It too bore the Olympic symbol. A large television screen hung from the ceiling flashing the exact time: 1:59:57 . . . 1:59:58 . . . 1:-59:59 . . . .

At precisely 2:00:00, the lights in the room dimmed. The curtain parted revealing a stage. On top of the stage stood a large, square box. It was an electronic computer. Its chrome knobs glistened. Its glass dials reflected the beams of twin spotlights.

"Gentlemen of the press," a voice boomed through the room. "Welcome to the future." The voice seemed to come from all sides.

22

"How about that," said one reporter, "a talking computer."

"Maybe it's the Wizard of Oz," said another.

Dave Henderson knew better, however. He recognized the voice as belonging to Peter Powell.

At that moment Peter Powell appeared on stage. He rested one hand on the computer. "Say hello to the press," instructed the Olympic chief.

Several lights on the computer flickered and a message flashed on the screen above. HELLO, it read. MY NAME IS PED-72.

"Would one of you like to ask PED-72 about its function?" prompted Powell.

"All right," snapped one voice. "What does it do?"

I AM THE OFFICIAL OLYMPIC COMPUTER, read the screen.

The crowd gasped. Dave's jaw dropped. This is too much, he thought.

"What is this," grumbled one of the reporters, "some kind of joke?"

"It's no joke," said Powell. "The Olympics have joined the computer age. This day has been coming for some years now. First came the photo-timer to decide races. Next came sighting devices to measure jumps and throws. PED-72 does all this—and more."

The computer screen flashed: I WILL JUDGE ALL OLYMPIC EVENTS.

There was a murmur of disbelief. Dave shook his head in disgust. He thought, What's the athletic world coming to—first Speed Sloan, and now *this!*

"I'm sure you've attended swimming or track meets where officials outnumbered athletes," stated Powell. "Or you've seen bad judging. Russian judges give American divers bad marks. And American judges score Russian gymnasts poorly. PED-72 will end that problem."

"I can see timing swimming races by computer," said the reporter. "But how do you judge diving? Or gymnastics?"

The Olympic chief just smiled. As though by command two youths in tights appeared. They dragged a mat before PED-72. On it they placed a sidehorse. One of the youths connected a wire attached to the sidehorse to the computer.

The second youth dusted his hands with powder and stood before the sidehorse. Suddenly he jumped upon it: whirling, spinning, twisting. He ended by landing stiff-legged on the mat.

PED-72's screen instantly flashed: GYMNAST 1 SCORES 22.3 POINTS.

The reporters gasped once again. "How does it work?" several asked.

A smile played across Powell's face. "Television cameras," he purred. "Sensor devices on the horse. Also under the mat. We programmed the computer. It knows how a champion gymnast would perform this routine. PED-72 can even tell you how an athlete scored or lost points."

As though the computer heard, its message screen flashed: GYMNAST 1 LOST BALANCE ON NO. 2

24

TWIST. 1.7 POINTS DEDUCTED FROM SCORE.
"No more bad judging," smirked Powell. "No arguments. The computer will decide all problems. What remains is pure sport."

Pure sport, thought Dave Henderson. What remains is mechanical sport. Why doesn't Powell program the athletes into the computer too? He recalled Dr. Costello's comment that Speed Sloan tested better than all his rivals. So why bother to run the race? They could do away with the Olympics. Everyone could stay home and keypunch their pulse rate into machines. The computer would award the gold medals.

Powell, however, continued to talk. He described how PED-72 would provide the press with data. Each seat in the press box would have its own screen. PED-72 would sell tickets. It would close the roof over the stadium in case of rain. The computer would even ignite the sky rockets at the closing ceremony.

Powell ended his speech, "Gentlemen, the Olympics of tomorrow are here today."

The lights in the room came back on. The press applauded. "Two more things," added the Olympic chief. "First, we will test the computer at the track meet this weekend. After that, it will be shipped overseas and installed in the Olympic stadium.

"Second, as you know, the Olympics are being held this summer in the small country of Scandia. The sponsors have asked the Olympic committee to add one more sport to the program—orienteering."

Powell didn't wait for further comment. He vanished from the stage. Dave and several other reporters moved forward to look more closely at the computer. "Orienteering?" Dave said to one of them. "What's that?"

Before the reporter could answer PED-72's screen flashed a message: ORIENTEERING COMBINES CROSS-COUNTRY RUNNING WITH MAP READING.

The swiftness of the reply startled Dave. "Oh, thanks," he said.

YOU'RE WELCOME, replied the computer. THIS MESSAGE COURTESY POWELL ELECTRONIC DEVICES.

CHAPTER 6 The morning after the press conference Dave went jogging with Larry through the woods. They followed a horse path beside a stream. The two jogged easily over its loose surface. Then crossing a road, they returned to the path on the other side.

Larry glanced over his shoulder. "Am I going too fast for you?" he said to the runner behind him.

"No," gasped Dave. "I'll survive."

The horse path ended and they moved onto a gravel road. Larry slowed, allowing Dave to catch up with him. They ran shoulder to shoulder.

"This is the kind of training I enjoy," said Larry. "Speed can stay on his treadmill. I like to get out into the woods."

"Doesn't Speed ever run cross-country," asked Dave. His voice sounded weak.

"He never gets out of sight of his stopwatch." Larry noticed his friend beginning to slow. "Come on, we'll walk awhile."

Dave sighed loudly. "Thanks," he said.

"Now you know how I feel trying to match Speed Sloan," commented Larry.

A car approached down the gravel road raising a cloud of dust. They moved aside to let it pass.

"I thought I was in good shape," said Dave. "I used to play basketball, but it's been a long time. I should run more often."

"You'll get there," said Larry. "Come on, let's jog some more."

They moved forward again at an easy pace. At the end of the gravel road they hopped a low fence and ran onto a golf course. The grass felt soft and spongy beneath Dave's feet.

They slowed to a walk once more. After Dave regained his breath, he asked Larry, "Have you ever heard of orienteering?"

"What's that?"

"It's a new sport they added to the Olympic program."

"Orienteering?" remarked Larry. "Sounds like something they invented in China."

"No, in Scandia," Dave corrected him. "I never heard of it before either, so I checked with my office. It's popular in Europe. Sometimes 5,000 people compete in a single orienteering meet. Men. Women. Boys. Girls. People in their sixties."

"How does it work?"

"It's part running and part map-reading," explained Dave. "You have a map that shows a number of checkpoints scattered throughout the woods. You have to locate the checkpoints using a compass. The fastest person to finish the course wins, but it takes brains as well as leg speed. If you like cross-country running, maybe you should try orienteering."

Larry laughed. "Have you ever seen me use a compass? When I was a boy scout, I went on a 14-mile hike. They had to use helicopters to find me."

The two began running once more. They ran down an asphalt road to the top of a high sand dune, then sprinted down the dune to the shore of a lake. The sand at the water's edge was wet and firm. Waves lapped at their feet.

They stopped again. Larry picked up a flat rock and skipped it three, four, five times across the water. "I wonder if it would be possible for someone like me to set a world's record?" he asked calmly.

Dave looked at Larry amused. "How?" he asked. "Climb on Speed's shoulders?"

"Maybe that would work," Larry said with a smile. "No, just find a loophole."

"You must be kidding."

"I'm not," said Larry. He picked up another rock. "I've been checking the rule book for loopholes." Larry threw the rock. It skipped lightly across the water. "Remember the catapult-shoe?"

Dave stopped and thought. As silly as it sounded, Larry might be right. Back in 1957 the Russians invented a jumping shoe with an inch-thick sole. "Catapult-shoe," the press called it. Yurij Stepanov used the shoe to break the world's high jump record. Nothing in the rules said you couldn't use such a shoe. It was a loophole. Later the shoe was outlawed.

The year before, in 1956, someone from Spain had invented a new way to throw a javelin. Most athletes ran straight down a runway before they threw. The Spanish thrower spun in a circle. He also soaped his hand to permit an easy release. The javelin flew forty feet past the world's record. Another loophole. Of course, they soon outlawed that style.

"You might get away with it—*once!*" said Dave. "Then they'd change the rules on you."

"I know," smiled Larry. He picked up another rock. "Just a crazy idea I got last night."

He threw the rock as hard as he could at the water. It went *bloomp* and sank from sight.

They started jogging again. As they ran back into the woods, Dave began to wonder what Larry had in mind.

CHAPTER 7

Ten thousand fans appeared at the track meet on Saturday. At first few of them noticed the computer, which occupied a place in the infield near the finish line. Dave did, however. He stood staring at the computer's dials, knobs, and switches. It seemed to him that the dials, knobs, and switches were staring back.

He also saw the large plate on the computer's face. *PED-72,* it read. *The official Olympic computer. Built by Powell Electronic Devices, Inc.*

Dave remembered that Peter Powell always gave

great speeches on the amateur code. The Olympic chief detested athletes who competed for money. "Pros have no part in the Olympic movement," Powell had stated in a recent newspaper interview. The Olympic committee once stripped Jim Thorpe of his medals, because the Indian decathlon champion accepted a few dollars for playing baseball. Dave wondered how many computers Peter Powell would sell following PED-72's use in the Olympics. A million dollars worth? Ten million? There seemed to be a double standard.

Dave reached for his camera. He walked around the computer deciding how to photograph the beast. He tried one or two shots from different angles. Finally he stopped.

"I guess if you've photographed one computer, you've photographed them all," he said to himself.

Bang! A pistol sounded from the other end of the track. The start of the 100-yard dash. The crowd snapped to its feet, craning to see as a half-dozen sprinters pounded down the straightaway.

Dave turned with his camera in time to catch a lean, black athlete straining for the tape.

At that instant the screen behind PED-72 glowed with letters and numbers: 1. BROOKS JOHNSON— 9:37 SECONDS. Then almost as quickly the computer flashed the names of the other finishers and their times to a hundredth of a second. Powell's machine worked all right.

The crowd applauded loudly. Dave couldn't tell whether they were cheering the runners or the machine

32

that had announced their times. The winning sprinter waved to the crowd and jogged back to the starting line for his sweats. The losers followed walking.

Powell sat in the front row of the grandstand. A smile creased his face at the proof of his computer's worth. Before PED-72 it would have taken a dozen judges and a dozen more men with stopwatches to get those results. And not that fast. He'll make fifty million dollars, decided Dave.

The crowd buzzed again with excitement. Speed Sloan had appeared on the track dressed in a sleek blue suit, a bag slung over one shoulder. The mile run would come next. Dave raised his camera and photographed Speed waving jauntily to the people in the stands.

Dr. Costello sat in Powell's box. The Olympic chief turned to the scientist. "How fast will your star pupil run today?"

"Four minutes," answered Costello. "We don't want to run him all out until the Olympic Games."

Powell nodded in agreement.

A half-dozen rows above Powell sat Stacy. She waved. "Good luck, Speed!" shouted the girl. The miler heard and glanced up. He simply raised four fingers in the air to show how fast he planned to run.

"He makes it seem so easy," Stacy commented to the girl sitting next to her. "It's almost unfair to the others."

Dave saw Stacy's greeting to Speed and frowned.

Speed crossed the track to the infield and dropped

his bag. He sat down on the Astroturf and began un-lacing his rubber-soled shoes. One of the judges passed. "World record today?" he asked.

"Not today," Speed replied. "Next month."

He reached inside the bag for a different pair of shoes, white with red stripes on each side. The bottoms had pinlike spikes for gripping the asphaltlike track. Dave had noticed the Simba shoe salesman in the stands earlier. But these were the other brand of shoes.

Dave kneeled nearby snapping one picture after another of Speed fastening his shoes. The runner glanced over at him. "You never quit, do you?"

"Nope," replied the photographer. "Never do."

Speed rose. He began to run warm-up sprints on the plastic grass. All eyes were focused on him. Larry Spitzig meanwhile entered the infield, but no one noticed. He sat alone changing his shoes. Dave glanced at him then returned his attention to Speed. Suddenly Dave almost dropped his camera. He realized what he had just seen.

He ran over to Larry. "What are you doing?"

"Just putting on my shoes," came the answer.

"Those aren't your shoes," said Dave. "Those are my shoes!" Indeed, Larry had donned Dave's roller shoes.

"Right."

"But you can't wear roller shoes in a track meet."

Larry looked up and a grin lit his face. He said a single word—"Loophole."

The loudspeaker crackled: "Last call for the mile."

Speed Sloan trotted onto the track. Larry rose and walked carefully after him. Nobody yet noticed that his shoes had ball bearings instead of spikes. Three other athletes joined them at the line.

The starter raised his pistol. "Take your marks." The gun sounded and the runners sped on their way.

All except Larry. Within the first step his feet slid out from under him. He landed on the track flat on his stomach. The crowd gasped.

The starter looked down at Larry, the pistol still in his hand. "What kind of shoes are those?"

Larry smiled up at him. "Don't shoot," he said, then scrambled to his feet. He started after the other four runners, who already had reached the turn.

The crowd looked at Larry moving with the sweeping stride of a skater. At first they seemed stunned. Then laughter rolled through the stands.

Peter Powell rose from his seat in the front row. His face blazed with anger. "He can't do that," raged the Olympic chief.

"Stop the race! Stop the race!" shouted Dr. Costello. But the race went on.

Stacy, sitting above them, said nothing. She just raised one hand to her mouth as though in shock.

Larry rolled down the backstretch moving faster now. Coming into the turn he caught the other runners. Their powerful legs beat the track, while he coasted behind them. On the straightaway, he pulled even with Speed. Speed glanced at him, still unaware of what was happening.

"Why aren't you setting pace?" Speed shouted at him. "Get out in front!"

"If you insist," said Larry. With several quick, gliding strokes, he moved quickly away from the champion runner.

"Hey, what is this?" shouted Speed, as Larry opened up a thirty-, then sixty-yard lead. The crowd roared with laughter. Peter Powell still stood in the front row.

"This is an outrage!" he cried.

Larry glided faster and faster. When he came past the stands again, the other runners had just reached the back turn. The crowd clapped their hands in rhythm urging him on. He circled the track once more. Coming into the final lap, he saw Speed Sloan and the other runners ahead of him. One by one he passed them again. On the final straightaway he rolled past Speed for the second time. He not only had beaten his rival but also had finished an entire lap ahead of him.

The crowd jumped and shouted with glee, but the electronic eyes of PED-72 also had watched the race. The computer's screen flashed as Larry crossed the line. MILE RUN WON BY LARRY SPITZIG. TIME 2:59:73.

"What?" asked Powell.

The machine continued: NEW WORLD RECORD. FORMER RECORD 3:51.1 BY JIM RYUN, USA.

"That's not true!" shouted Powell.

PED-72, however, rolled on: LARRY SPITZIG NOT ONLY SET A WORLD RECORD FOR THE MILE, BUT HE BECOMES THE FIRST RUNNER TO BETTER THREE MINUTES.

"Stop that machine!" snapped the Olympic chief. "Turn it off!" He started down out of the stands. Dr. Costello trailed at his heels.

ROGER BANNISTER OF GREAT BRITAIN WAS FIRST TO BETTER FOUR MINUTES. HE RAN 3:59.6 IN 1954, read PED-72.

Powell stood now before his computer. "You can't say that. He wore roller skates instead of shoes." He angrily pointed a finger at Larry. "Disqualify him!"

The machine replied: I AM SORRY. I AM NOT PROGRAMMED TO HONOR THAT REQUEST.

The Olympic chief pulled the plug out of his machine, silencing it. He stalked off.

At that moment Speed Sloan crossed the finish line. He had run his race in four minutes, only to finish second. Speed went directly to his track bag in the infield and picked it up. He glared at Larry as the two passed.

Larry sat down in the grass to remove his roller shoes. Suddenly Dr. Costello was standing over him. "Why you—" stammered the doctor. "You'll never set foot on one of my treadmills again!" He turned to follow Powell.

Stacy next appeared. She also seemed disturbed. "Where did you get those skates?"

Larry didn't say anything, but glanced guiltily toward Dave Henderson. Stacy turned toward the photographer. Suddenly Dave's face grew very red.

"Did you—" began Stacy. She seemed angry. "Did you—" she repeated. Suddenly she began to grin. "Did you see the look on Speed's face when Larry skated past him?"

Dave smiled with relief.

"I'll tell you what Speed looked like," Larry said, starting to chuckle. "He looked just like Stacy's stainless steel frog."

The three of them spent the next five minutes laughing until tears came to their eyes.

CHAPTER 8

The *Sports Weekly* offices buzzed with the sound of people working. It was several days after the track meet. Dave entered the photo lab carrying an envelope under one arm. He flipped a switch on the light box and placed a number of color transparencies on the glass.

Dave bent forward to study the pictures taken during the week with Speed. It was all there, captured forever by the camera. There were pictures of Speed at the airport; Speed on the treadmill; Speed running lap after lap against the stopwatch; and finally Speed being beaten by Larry wearing roller skates.

Larry's mile record lasted only twenty-four hours. The next morning Peter Powell announced that the world track officials had voted to outlaw roller skates. One more loophole had been plugged.

Dave stared at the transparencies. Dull, he thought. Dave had hoped the magazine might use one of his pictures on the cover. He had never made the cover of *Sports Weekly* before. But he had nothing but very dull pictures. Very dull Speed. Between treadmills and computers, the fun seemed to be vanishing from sports. Even the Olympics seemed on its way to becoming nothing but big business.

Nevertheless, Dave wanted to go to the Olympics this summer. He had sent a memo yesterday to managing editor Andy Creighton. The memo outlined a story idea. If he could get to Scandia, it would help his career. And his idea might restore some fun to the Olympic Games. Besides, he could see Stacy again.

The telephone rang. Dave reached for the receiver. "The chief wants to see you," said a woman's voice.

"Right," answered Dave.

Stuffing the color transparencies back in the envelope, Dave turned off the light box. He left the photo lab and walked down a long corridor, passing a display case. A Greek vase stood inside. *Sports Weekly* awarded the vase each year to its "Sportsman of the Year." Dave groaned thinking that should Speed Sloan win at the Olympics, the vase might go to him.

Andrew Creighton, managing editor of *Sports Weekly,* sat awaiting Dave. The editor peered over a pair of horn-rimmed glasses and put a cigar out in an ashtray. He glanced at the memo Dave had sent him. "So, Henderson. You want to go to the Olympics?"

"That's correct," Dave answered. "I think it would make a great story."

"I've never heard of orienteering in the Olympics before," said the editor. He tapped the memo with a forefinger. "What do you mean by 'exhibition' sport?"

Dave explained, "Each four years the home country selects one or more exhibition sports. There are no official entries. They award medals, but not the regular Olympic gold, silver, and bronze medals. It simply permits the home country to display a locally popular sport. In 1964 the Japanese chose baseball. Four years later the Mexicans picked fronton tennis."

Creighton rose from his desk and walked to the window. He stared down at the cars and people far below. "I recall that now," said the editor. "A couple of Philadelphia businessmen . . ."

Dave smiled. The editor already was ahead of him. Before the Mexicans added fronton tennis to the 1968 Olympic program, nobody played that game in the United States. Nevertheless, several businessmen from Philadelphia decided they wanted to go to the Olympics and play fronton tennis. And they had entered as the American team. They lost, of course, but at least they took part. And wasn't that the Olympic ideal—at least before treadmills and computers.

"You want to form a team with this Larry Spitzig," said the editor. "Isn't that the kid who raced a three-minute mile on roller skates?"

Dave nodded.

Creighton chuckled. "Heck of a trick. I would have loved to have seen that stuffed shirt Powell's face. But won't Powell block this kid from the team?"

"Powell won't know," explained Dave. "It's only a so-called local sport. It's very popular in Scandia, but Scandia is a small country. There's no money in it. So the Olympic committee doesn't care. We can enter directly with the Scandian officials. Probably nobody else from the United States will think to enter as an orienteering team. If so, we're home free."

"Beautiful idea," said Creighton. "It'll give us a good story and help poke some fun at those people who think just because somebody on their side wins a gold medal, that makes their country better than everyone else's.

"Okay, you're on. We'll just add you to our photo staff for the games—but you'll have to work."

Dave started for the door. "One more thing," the editor called after him. "Just hope they don't hear of orienteering in Philadelphia."

Dave strode out of the office smiling broadly. He'd have to make a phone call. There was a rabbit friend of his who would need to know he had just been picked for the American Olympic team.

42

CHAPTER 9

"Are you kidding?" Larry laughed when Dave called with the plan to go to the Olympic Games as orienteers. "Wait until Speed Sloan finds out about this. Wait until Powell finds out."

Speed didn't hear the news until several days later. Stacy informed him one night after practice. Speed mumbled several angry words, then stalked away. "Speed's an old prune," Stacy said later when she described the incident to her cousin.

"Yeah," Larry agreed.

During the weeks before the Olympics, Larry and

Dave practiced as orienteers. Any worries about the reaction of Peter Powell faded when the Olympic Village opened in Scandia toward the end of the summer. The two orienteers disappeared easily into the crowd of nearly 10,000 athletes assembled for the games.

The Olympic Village functioned like a city within a city. It contained eating halls, shops, theaters, a post office, and practice fields. Buses transported the athletes to scattered playing sites in the Scandian capital city. The stadium for track and field was on one side of town. The swim palace was on the other. Orienteers would compete in the large woods behind the Olympic Village.

Day and night crowds of Scandian men, women, children, babies, and dogs flocked to the village on the edge of town. They stared through the fence at the athletes inside. They waved, and shouted, and called their heroes by name. Sometimes the athletes waved back, but a water-filled moat inside the fence prevented them from getting close to each other. It made Dave Henderson feel like a monkey in the zoo.

Machines outside the fence provided sports fans with souvenirs. Drop a coin in the slot, say the name of your favorite hero, and an autographed picture appeared—courtesy of PED-72.

In the week before the start of the Olympic Games, nearly 14,000 people asked for pictures of the famous American miler, Speed Sloan. About half that number wanted pictures of Sloan's number one rival, the African runner, Andrew Martin. Only three had requested pictures of Dave Henderson.

Dave knew the figures because he had asked the computer that morning. Each room in the village contained a TV screen connected to PED-72. You could ask it questions. You could see any sport in progress. You could even order your dinner.

Dave tapped the keyboard beside his bed. Within seconds the face of Larry Spitzig filled the screen. "Fellow orienteer," said Larry when he saw who was calling.

"Larry, I'm going down to the practice track to take some pictures," said Dave. "Want to come along?"

"I'm a bit tired from today's workout," Larry replied. "I'm going to rest until the opening ceremony."

"Okay, see you later." Dave tapped the keyboard again. Larry's face vanished from the screen.

Dave selected a camera from his desk and hung it around his neck. It had an ordinary fifty-millimeter lens. He debated for a moment about whether or not to bring along a telephoto lens. Finally he decided against it. He would travel light today and work on close-up shots. He stuffed a half-dozen boxes of film in his pocket and walked to the door. It slid automatically open as he approached, then closed after he had gone through.

The elevator started down at once, almost as though it knew where Dave was going. Well, maybe it did. Dave had told Larry. The computer had heard. It probably stored the information in its memory bank.

Dave gazed upward at the elevator's TV monitor. Suddenly on impulse he asked, "What's my name?"

DAVE HENDERSON, the monitor read.

"Just checking," mumbled Dave. He stepped outside and onto a moving sidewalk. It glided smoothly toward the practice running track.

The track buzzed with action. At least two dozen athletes practiced their events. A mammoth Russian wearing a red jersey stood in a circle balancing a shot in one hand. He coiled, exploded, and the round ball arched into the air. But a buzzer sounded. The Russian's foot had slid outside the circle. The judging machine sensed it and had signaled a foul.

Nearby a Japanese vaulter streaked down a runway and thrust his pole into a box. The fiberglass pole bent almost double and catapulted him up and over a bar 14-feet off the ground. He fell downward onto a plastic cushion that went *vloomp* when he landed. Then the vaulter picked up his pole and walked to a nearby TV monitor. He pushed a button and the monitor showed an instant replay of the vault.

At one end of the track, three sprinters from different countries used an electronic device to practice starts. The machine's voice barked the starting commands. A buzzer sounded. The sprinters burst from their blocks pounding the track for thirty or forty yards. Then they returned and examined the device. It told them to within a thousandth of a second how quickly they had reacted to the gun.

Dave, watching all this, cynically decided that nothing was left to chance any longer.

He walked toward the straightaway to see Speed Sloan practicing. Several dozen reporters and photographers stood watching him. Speed was running with another American runner, Jim Price. Supposedly Price was Sloan's new "rabbit."

Dr. Costello stood nearby pointing a sonar device at Speed as he jogged easily around the track. It was a new machine just developed by the scientist. The device measured Speed's heartbeat. When his heartbeat slowed to a certain level, the doctor signaled. The runner would then begin another fast lap. This went on and on until finally Speed's heartbeat showed him too tired to continue. Dr. Costello packed his device and left.

Dave glanced across the track and noticed the Simba shoe salesman nearby. He still had his suitcase. Obviously, the man had failed to convert Speed to Simba shoes. Speed still wore his old brand.

Dave also noticed Stacy Randolph walking back to the dormitory. She probably had just come from diving practice. He waved at her and she waved back.

Speed jogged a half-dozen more laps to cool down, then stopped to don his sweatsuit. The reporters and photographers gathered around him in a circle. Dave joined the crowd. Speed glanced up, his eyes flashing angrily. "Still taking pictures, huh?"

"Never stop," said Dave smiling.

Speed didn't return the smile. "How's your friend with the roller skates doing as an orienteer?"

"Well, we found out that roller skates don't work too well out in the woods."

"You clowns think this is funny, don't you?"

47

snapped Speed. "I've worked four years to prepare for these Olympics. You haven't trained even four weeks. What right do you have to be on an Olympic team?"

Before Dave could respond, a large whoop sounded at the other end of the track. "Good grief," said Dave. "What's that?"

"That's Andrew Martin," commented one of the reporters. "He always gives his battle cry when he steps onto the track. He claims it worries the other runners."

"It doesn't worry me," snapped Speed. Nevertheless, he turned to look. An African runner wearing a bright, yellow and red sweatsuit moved toward them. He ran barefoot. Most sports writers believed that of all the runners entered in the 1500 meters, only Martin had a chance to beat Speed Sloan.

Dave raised his camera and focused it on the new figure approaching. "Look at him," sneered Speed. "He doesn't even wear shoes."

"Well, you won't have to worry about him beating you with roller skates," said Dave.

The African bounded gazellelike through the grass. When he came near, one of the reporters shouted, "Hey Martin, have you met Speed Sloan?"

The African paused and a broad grin swept his face. He offered his hand. Speed accepted it.

"How about a shot of you two standing together," shouted one of the reporters.

"Look at each other not the camera," instructed another.

48

"Say something to him, Speed," said a photographer.

"Yeah," said the first reporter. "Can you speak Swahili?"

Speed looked puzzled as though not sure what to say to his rival. "You . . . run," Speed began, speaking slowly and loudly, ". . . 1500 meters?"

The African grinned even more broadly.

"You," asked Speed pointing at the other runner, ". . . like Olympics?" He made a sweeping movement with one hand as if to take in the entire Olympic Village.

Andrew Martin suddenly roared with laughter. "Really, fellow," he said. "I think you've seen too many Tarzan movies."

Speed Sloan's face turned red. "I see you know how to speak English," the American runner said icily.

"Forgive these chaps," said the African, motioning toward the reporters. "They're joking with you. They know I learned English in school."

Speed Sloan quickly turned away. He picked up his shoes. Dave could see Speed was angry at being made a fool. As he walked away, Speed shouted over his shoulder, "We'll see how much you're laughing at the finish line of the 1500 meters."

CHAPTER 10 The following day Larry and Dave practiced orienteering in the woods behind the Olympic Village. They stood on top of a hill gazing all around them. "The checkpoint should be right here," said Dave, "but I don't see it."

Finally Larry shouted, "There it is!" Dave looked toward where Larry pointed. A red flag fluttered on the *next* hill. They finally had found the checkpoint.

The two began running toward it. Orienteering seemed easier than when they arrived at the village two weeks ago. Together they ran the practice course fairly well. Apart was disaster. Dave ran too slowly; Larry read the compass too poorly. He might take a compass reading and wind up going 180 degrees the wrong way. And they had only a few days in which to improve.

They climbed the next hill and stopped under the flag. Dave placed his map on a flat rock and put the compass on top of it. He moved the map to orient it.

"That way," said Dave, pointing. "That's our next checkpoint."

At that moment they heard a noise in the woods. "What's that?" asked Larry.

"Probably another orienteer," said Dave.

"What if it's a tiger? I told you to bring a hunting rifle."

"Tigers?" said Dave. "In Scandia?"

But it was neither orienteer nor tiger. Andrew Martin appeared jogging through the brush. They shouted hello and he stopped. "Don't halt your workout just for us," Dave advised.

"I'm just off for an easy jaunt through the woods," explained the African runner. "I need to relax before the 1500-meter heats tomorrow." Andrew noticed their map and compass. "You must be orienteers."

"We're trying to be," said Dave. He showed the African their map and pointed out the next checkpoint.

"How do you plan to get there?" asked the African.

"Run straight at it, I guess," said Larry.

Andrew Martin shook his head. "Look, I'll show you a better way. Sometimes the shortest distance between two points is not a straight line." The African picked up the map. "See here," he said, pointing to a path zigzagging through the woods. It circled behind the next checkpoint.

"He's right," said Dave. "We'll cover more distance, but get there in less time."

"Come on," said Andrew. "I'll go with you." He led, running with an easy, loping gait. They located the path and followed its zigs and zags. Finally they cut back through the brush and up a long slope. Sure enough, they saw another red flag.

"That seemed easy," said Dave.

"Just a trick I picked up."

"Were you born—" Dave began.

"In the jungle?" the African finished the question. "No. No. I lived all my life in a city of 100,000 people. We have streets and tall buildings just like Chicago or New York. Maybe not so many. I learned to use a map and compass in the army."

Dave chose another compass reading. Using Andrew's hint, they picked a ravine to run along. The three runners found the next checkpoint almost at once. It seemed much easier that way. They ran for another half hour before returning to the village.

Dave and Larry waved goodbye to Andrew Martin, wishing him luck in tomorrow's race. They walked the rest of the way to their apartment building.

"Boy, would I love to see Andrew Martin beat Speed Sloan," said Larry.

"So would I," Dave agreed.

Then they climbed inside an elevator. Without their even pushing a button, it whisked them quickly up to their rooms.

CHAPTER 11 The next afternoon Dave stood before a door marked "Press" and spoke his name. There was a short pause while the sensor device decided whether or not to admit him.

The door hummed open. Dave walked through it into an area of the stadium reserved for photographers. He carried a bag containing his camera gear.

Eighty thousand people jammed the Olympic stadium. The quarterfinals in the 1500-meter run would occur later that afternoon—four heats. The first four finishers in each heat would run in one of two semifinal races tomorrow. Eight finalists would run for the gold medal on the third day.

Andrew Martin was in heat one today; Speed Sloan in heat four.

Dave began to unpack his gear. He unfolded a tripod and attached to it a camera with a long telephoto lens. Sighting through the lens, Dave could look right down the straightaway. The runners coming off the turn would be in perfect focus. As they neared the finish, he could shift to a second camera, which he had around his neck. He also had placed his remote control camera on the far side of the track. He could fire it by radio signal.

Dave felt a tap on his shoulder. "Do you know those people?" asked one of the other cameramen. He pointed to the next section of the stadium.

Dave glanced to his right. Larry Spitzig and Stacy Randolph sat nearby. They were smiling and waving at him.

"How did the diving go today?" Dave shouted.

"I made the finals," replied Stacy. She held her good luck frog overhead.

Dave grinned. "See you after the last race." The two nodded.

The crowd stirred. The finals in the 110-meter high hurdles race were about to begin. Dave looked down toward the track. Ten rows of hurdles began to rise, as if by magic. At the same time, a section of the plastic infield grass slid aside. An elevator lifted eight long-legged hurdlers into view. The crowd cheered.

In the race a runner from the United States leaned first into the light beam that served as the finish tape. He won by inches.

The American stood on a platform to accept his gold medal from Peter Powell. The "Star Spangled Banner" played through stereophonic speakers. The giant screen at one end of the stadium flashed an American flag. The screen at the other end showed a picture of the red, white, and blue-uniformed runner straining toward victory. Dave took a deep breath of air-conditioned air and felt proud.

The day's events continued. The athletes gracefully ran, jumped, and threw. PED-72 faithfully recorded their efforts in hundredths of seconds and thousandths of meters. Millions of people all over the world watched on their television screens.

Finally it came time for the 1500-meter heats. As had others before them, the runners of the first heat of the 1500-meter race had warmed up by jogging on treadmills in the stadium basement. Andrew Martin was among them. Now the elevator lifted them to the track. The crowd hushed and a buzzer sounded signaling the start of the race.

The runners pounded down the back straightaway fighting for the inside lane. Dave reached for his radio control box. He pushed the button to fire his camera on the far side of the stadium. *Click.* Then as the runners came out of the turn, he shifted to his telephoto camera. He sighted down the straightaway. *Click. Click. Click.*

Andrew Martin had started slowly and now ran

56

last. As the field moved into the second lap, the African runner slowly moved up in the pack. An electronic buzzer sounded at the start of the last lap and Martin took the lead. In the last hundred yards, however, he saw he would qualify easily and relaxed. Two other runners moved up to cross the line even with him. A fourth runner, two strides behind, also qualified for the semifinals.

Dave glanced over toward Larry. His friend raised a clenched fist as a sign of victory.

The American Jim Price won the second heat. The third race went to a short blond runner from Sweden. Then came Speed Sloan's heat. Speed removed his sweatsuit and stood behind the starting line in his blue jersey and red shorts.

Dave lowered his camera. Something look different about Speed today. He tried to decide what, but had no time. The gun sounded.

Speed moved easily off the line falling in near the rear of the pack as had Andrew Martin. As the runners swept into the first turn Dave again pushed the button on his radio control box. *Click.* Speed Sloan took control of the race toward the end of the second lap. He won going away.

The crowd began leaving the large stadium. Dave packed his gear and moved to where Larry and Stacy waited. "Did you notice Speed?" Larry commented.

"He won," Dave replied puzzled.

"No, his shoes," said Larry. "They were gold. Speed wore Simba shoes."

At once Dave realized what had seemed strange

about Speed standing at the starting line. He never had used that brand of shoe before. Dave recalled Larry's theory that the Simba salesman was trying to get Speed to switch.

"You don't suppose Speed's getting paid," suggested Stacy.

"It's happened before," said Larry.

"But he could lose his Olympic medal for accepting money," said Stacy. "That is—if he wins one."

Larry shrugged.

"Listen," Dave said. "We can discuss this later. I need to retrieve my remote control camera."

"I'll go with you," said Stacy.

Larry noticed how pleased Dave seemed and decided to leave the two and return to the village alone. Dave and Stacy walked down a ramp to the track. They showed their badges to the guard and crossed the plastic infield grass to get Dave's camera.

He picked it up in his hands and frowned.

"What's wrong?" asked Stacy.

"It didn't take any pictures," Dave replied. "That's never happened before." He examined the camera and pressed the button. *Click. Click.* It worked now, but somehow the radio control had failed. There was nothing he could do at the moment, so Dave started to pack it in his case.

As he did so, Stacy glanced over his shoulder. "What is that?" she asked pointing at another camera in his case. "Isn't that an awfully long lens?"

"It's a telephoto," Dave explained. "It's like looking through a telescope. You can shoot pictures from far away. For example, see those two people in that passage at the other end of the track?"

"Just barely," replied Stacy. "I can't tell who they are."

"I could photograph them and it would look like they were standing next to us."

"I don't believe it," said Stacy.

"Here, I'll show you," Dave said and raised the camera to his eye. He focused it on the two people. Suddenly his eyebrows arched in surprise. One of them was Speed Sloan. What was he doing?

"What's the matter?" Stacy asked.

"Nothing," Dave said. "Nothing." But he quickly snapped a picture. And he kept on snapping them until the film ran out in his camera.

"You act as though something was wrong, Dave."

"I just want to get back to the village," the photographer replied. "I want to see Larry when he returns. We have something to talk about."

CHAPTER 12 The following morning Dave bent over a work table in the Olympic Village darkroom. He gently jiggled a tray in his hands. Larry stood beside him.

The clear liquid in the tray rippled across a piece of white paper. Then slowly shadows appeared on the paper. The shadows became people. A clear picture appeared. Dave picked the wet photograph out of the tray and flattened it on a metal plate. He snapped on an overhead light.

The photograph showed Speed Sloan standing at

one end of the track talking to a man. It was one of the pictures Dave had snapped after the 1500-meter trials the day before. Speed seemed to be accepting an envelope, but the other man's face was lost in the shadows.

"Do you think it's the Simba shoe salesman?" asked Larry.

"It might be him," said Dave. "But even if it is, that doesn't prove anything."

"What if Speed accepted money for wearing Simba shoes?"

"There's not much we can do about it," Dave replied, "at least not with these pictures."

Dave glanced at his watch. Nearly ten o'clock. He wanted to get over to the swimming pool to see Stacy dive. He quickly dried the last photograph and stuffed it with several others in a large envelope.

"What are you going to do with the photos?" asked Larry.

"We'll take them up to my room," said Dave. "I don't want anyone else to find them."

After leaving the photographs, Dave and Larry returned down the elevator. They mounted the moving sidewalk that took them to the bus depot. Within a short time they had arrived at the swim palace.

It was the last heat of the 400-meter dash for men. The swimmers churned through the water, turning it white with their kicking. A tall boy in red trunks moved into the lead. At the far end of the pool he somersaulted, pushing off against the side with

61

his feet. Stroking quickly he pulled away from the other swimmers. He slapped at the pool's edge with his final stroke.

Flash! A spotlight lit his lane. It marked him as the winner. In the same instant, his name, country, and time appeared on the scoreboard. As each of the other seven swimmers touched, their names also appeared. The fans applauded.

"Peter Powell strikes again," commented Dave.

"If PED-72 ever blows a fuse," said Larry, "they'll have to close the Olympics and go home."

Dave shook his head in wonderment.

The loudspeaker announced: "The next event will be women's platform diving."

The fans looked toward the other end of the building. The swim palace contained a second pool only for diving. The diving pool had a half-dozen boards of all heights. A tall platform reached almost to the roof. It stood ten-meters high—more than thirty feet.

Some of the girls already had begun their practice dives. They rode an elevator to the top of the platform. They paused. Then they stood still as posts. Finally they launched themselves into space, spinning, twisting, until they knifed into the blue waters below.

Peter Powell's electronic device watched. Sensor cameras followed each spin and twist. Cameras had even been placed beneath the surface of the water. The cameras flashed their data to PED-72. The computer then compared the dive to its memory picture of what would be a perfect dive. Before the diver popped to the surface, her score flashed on the board.

Stacy finished her practice dives. She sat on a bench by the side of the pool waiting for the event to begin. Dave called to her. When she looked up, he shouted, "Good luck!"

"Thanks, I'll need it," she yelled back.

"Got your frog?"

Stacy pointed to the shiny object by her feet.

The diving began. Forty-three girls had entered from all over the world. Each would take three dives and be scored for those dives. The top twelve scorers would dive in the finals on the two following days.

On the first day of the finals they would take three required dives. On the next day they could select three dives of their own choice. The more difficult the dive, the better the dive, the more points they scored. The girl with the highest number of points would become Olympic champion.

One by one the girls mounted the platform for their first dives. As they did, PED-72 recorded their scores. A girl from East Germany smoothly did a back two-and-a-half somersault and scored eighty-one out of a possible hundred points. A Japanese diver tried a forward three-and-a-half somersault and earned seventy-nine points.

Then Stacy appeared on the top of the platform. She bent over and placed her steel frog near the edge.

"I wonder what the computer thinks of frogs?" Dave asked Larry.

"I'm not programmed to answer that question," Larry replied.

Stacy stood still for a moment. Then she took two short steps and bounced into the air. Her body turned once, twice, then a half, and finally a full twist. She sliced knifelike into the water. The crowd gasped.

"Beautiful dive!" Larry shouted, clapping his hands.

"Look at the scoreboard," said Dave.

The scoreboard credited Stacy with seventy-four points. Larry frowned. "I thought she dived better than that."

"The computer never lies," growled Dave.

At the end of the day's diving, Stacy ranked sixth. She made the finals. But when she walked over to talk to Dave and Larry, she seemed sad.

"I feel good," said the girl. "I can't understand why I'm not scoring higher."

"These scores won't count in the finals," Dave advised. "You'll do better tomorrow."

"I hope so," she said.

After Stacy dressed, the three took the bus back to the Olympic Village. They ate in the cafeteria and sat for several hours watching the Olympic fencing matches on television.

The athletes fenced with electric cords attached to their belts. When one of them scored a hit, an electric light flashed. It was nearly ten o'clock before the two reached Dave's room.

He knew at once something was wrong. "They're gone," he said to Larry.

"What's gone?"

"The photographs," said Dave. "Someone came in here and stole them."

"But who?"

Dave said nothing.

Larry snapped his fingers. "Speed Sloan!"

"Perhaps," Dave replied.

"He must know we saw him talking with the Simba shoe man."

Dave thought for a minute. "We don't have any proof," he finally said. "About all we can do now is wait. Let's go to bed." The orienteering events began the next day and Dave wanted all the sleep he could get.

CHAPTER 13

"Go!" shouted the official at the starting line. He removed his hand from Larry Spitzig's shoulder, and the young runner started off down the hill. In one hand he carried his map. In the other, a compass.

Larry sprinted down the hill for a hundred yards until he reached a bulletin board. On it was tacked a large map similar to the one in his hand. The large map showed the checkpoints on the orienteering course. Larry copied them, then was off running through the woods.

"Run hard!" Dave Henderson shouted after him. But maybe he should have said, *"Read* hard." Larry had more trouble reading the compass than he did running.

Dave waited near the starting line for his turn. A dozen other orienteers stood before him. Each minute another one would rush off the line.

"Go!" shouted the official, and one more athlete started down the hill. By that time Larry had vanished.

Finally Dave stood on the line. The official's hand gripped his shoulder. At that point Dave realized he had become an Olympic athlete. He was running for his country in the world's number one sporting event —the Olympic Games. A shudder passed through his body.

But Dave had no more time to worry. The official's hand lifted from his shoulder. "Go!"

Dave ran down the hill to the bulletin board. It showed the ten checkpoints, marked on the map in red ink. He quickly copied them onto his own map. He drew lines connecting each one. Then he laid his compass on the map next to the first line. The compass pointed to a tall tree at the edge of the woods. Dave started toward it, but at a much slower pace than Larry.

The woods quickly swallowed him. He checked his compass once more. Eighty thousand people would jam the main Olympic stadium that day for the semifinal heats of the 1500-meter run. They wanted to see Speed Sloan, and Andrew Martin. But no fans could see

Dave, or Larry, or the other orienteers in their event. Perhaps it worked better that way.

Halfway up a long hill, Dave had to walk. Once over the crest he looked down and spotted the red flag marking the first checkpoint. He quickly ran to it.

Using the rubber stamp dangling beneath the flag, Dave marked his card. This would prove he had found the checkpoint. Dave smiled. Several weeks ago Peter Powell had offered to wire the checkpoints into PED-72. The orienteers could be checked electronically. But the orienteering people politely told Powell no. They wanted to keep their event as simple as possible.

Dave checked his map. He found a footpath that passed near the second checkpoint. Remembering Andrew Martin's advice, he decided to follow the path. He sighted with his compass and started toward it.

At that moment a noise startled him. Dave looked over his shoulder in time to see a second runner crashing through the brush toward him. The runner waved his map board and shouted a greeting in a strange language.

"Keep it up!" Dave yelled back. The runner soon vanished from sight. Dave started to walk. He bent to rub his legs, which he had scraped in the bushes.

He began running again, and soon found the second checkpoint. By then, two more runners had charged past him. Dave realized he would win no gold medal today.

He checked his compass again and started for

checkpoint three. Finding that easily, he moved onto the fourth. Dave had no trouble reading his map or compass. But he ran slowly, and he stopped often to walk.

Finally Dave sighted the finish line ahead. He tried to move faster, but his legs wouldn't let him. In the last few yards another runner sprinted past him. He crossed the line and walked slowly to the table to hand in his card.

The official checked the card and smiled. "Well, you found all ten."

Dave leaned against the table and smiled back weakly. He had found all the checkpoints, but his time was very slow. Still, he felt pleased with himself.

Sitting down in the grass, Dave started to rub his legs. Several other orienteers stopped to shake his hand. He still hadn't spotted Larry. But he saw Stacy moving toward him.

"Why are you rubbing your legs?" asked the girl. "Do they hurt that much?"

"They itch," he replied. "Where's Larry?"

"He hasn't come across the line yet," answered Stacy.

Dave frowned. Could Larry have gotten lost. At that moment Dave realized that Stacy must have come direct to the orienteering race from the diving. "How were your first three dives?" he asked.

"Not too good," answered the girl. "Well, the dives felt good, but the scores were poor. I'm in fourth place."

"Strange," said Dave.

At that instant, a long silver limousine bearing the American flag appeared on the road. It stopped and a uniformed guard opened the rear door. Peter Powell stepped out followed by Dr. Costello. "Well, how are my boys doing?" he asked.

"One American just finished," commented an official pointing toward the scoreboard.

Powell glanced at where it said: DAVE HENDERSON, USA. He compared the time next to that name with the other times on the board. Powell grimaced. Then he looked down toward where Dave sat, as though expecting an excuse.

Dave grinned up at him. "I think I've got poison ivy," he said. He suspected that Powell had come to the orienteering meet only to gloat over their plight.

"And where is your teammate?" sneered Powell.

"I'm afraid he's lost," Dave replied.

Powell shook his head slowly. "It was a sad day for the United States when you two joined the Olympic team. Fortunately we have Speed Sloan to make people forget you."

Suddenly Stacy shouted, "Look, it's Larry." They turned in time to see the young runner cross the finish line.

He dropped his card on the scoring table. "I guess I didn't have a very good day," he said.

The scorer looked at the card. "You missed half the checkpoints."

"Like I said," repeated Larry. "I guess I didn't have a very good day."

Peter Powell moved toward the runner. "It seems your roller skates don't work in the woods." For a moment Dave thought he was going to strike Larry. But Powell stalked off to his limousine. Dr. Costello started to leave with him.

Costello opened the door for Powell. Just before the Olympic chief got in, he turned again to Larry and Dave. "You two are a disgrace to the American flag!" Then he drove off in the gathering dusk.

CHAPTER 14 After Powell had left, Dave glanced at his watch. "Holy cow," he said. "It's late."

"What's wrong?" asked Stacy.

"I'm supposed to be at the stadium taking pictures," he answered. "The 1500-meter semifinals are in ten minutes." He began jogging up the road toward the main highway.

Stacy and Larry started after him. "Wait for us," she called.

At the highway they waited several minutes hoping to see a taxi. Finally a bus marked "Olympic Stadium" appeared. The three climbed aboard.

Five minutes later they arrived at the huge circular stadium. Dave entered the press elevator. "I'll see you after the races," he told the others.

When Dave reached his place in the stands, he found that one of the other *Sports Weekly* reporters had expected him to be late. "I've got your cameras ready," said the reporter, "including your remote unit on the other side of the track."

The meet progressed swiftly. As expected, Speed Sloan won his heat in the 1500 meters by more than ten yards. In heat two, Andrew Martin ran easily settling for second place behind the other American, Jim Price. The big clash would come between Sloan and Martin in the finals the following day.

Following the last race Dave met Larry and Stacy again. They descended to the track to check his remote control camera. To his dismay, he discovered the camera had failed again. He tested his radio unit once more. *Click-click-click* went the camera.

"It works down here," Dave complained. "What's wrong with my radio signal?"

"Maybe there's too much other electronic gear in the stadium," suggested Larry.

"You might be right," said Dave. "With all this gadgetry, there may be interference. What I need is a stronger signal. I'll rig up a different antenna for tomorrow."

They headed through a tunnel beneath the stands to where an athletes' bus waited. Andrew Martin sat in the first seat. They congratulated him. "Good race today."

"Thank you," said the African smiling. "How about you two."

Dave shook his head. "It just isn't our day. My camera failed to work, and Larry got lost in the woods."

At that moment Speed Sloan climbed onto the bus. "Well, if it isn't the stars of our orienteering team," he sneered.

"You're not cute, Speed," Stacy snapped at him.

The miler ignored her and turned instead to Larry. "What's the matter? Trip in a rabbit hole?"

Larry cringed. Speed headed toward the back of the bus laughing.

"He may or may not be the world's fastest miler," said Stacy, "but he's certainly the world's biggest creep."

The bus headed toward the Olympic Village. "I don't know what went wrong," Larry said to Andrew Martin. "I thought I was getting good with the compass."

"Maybe it's not you," said Andrew.

"What do you mean by that?" asked Dave. The African merely held one finger aloft as though telling him to wait.

The bus halted at the Olympic Village and everyone got off. "Now," said the African. "Let me see your compass."

The three gathered around him. He stood pointing the compass toward the setting sun. The compass needle vibrated before stopping at about a sixty degree angle. "There's your answer," said Andrew. "This compass should be pointing at ninety degrees. It's not."

"Look at that," said Dave. As they watched, the compass needle suddenly shifted several more degrees.

"Maybe all these electronic gadgets affect it," suggested Larry.

"We can't blame everything on PED-72," said Dave. He pulled his compass out. Its needle pointed directly north.

"Someone's tampered with Larry's compass," Stacy realized.

"I'd be willing to bet," announced Dave, "that whoever fooled with this compass also stole the pictures we developed this morning."

Speed had just climbed down from the bus carrying a small bag. Their eyes turned toward him. "What do you know about Larry's compass?" challenged Stacy.

"About as much as he does," sneered Speed, "which isn't much."

Larry turned toward the miler. "What was in that envelope the Simba salesman handed you yesterday?" he asked.

Speed suddenly flushed. "What are you talking about?"

"He's saying, you accepted money for wearing Simba shoes," said Stacy.

Speed glared angrily at the girl, then started to leave. "You can't prove a thing," he shouted over his shoulder.

"What is all this?" asked Andrew Martin after Speed had left. They quickly told him.

The African listened intently, nodding. Then he smiled, "If all this is true, I know a way to get even with both the shoe salesman and your friend, the speedy Mister Sloan."

"What do you suggest?" asked Larry. "Shall we set a trap for them?"

"Oh, nothing as crude as that," laughed the African. "I was simply thinking how funny it would be if the winner of the 1500-meter run were someone who ran barefoot."

CHAPTER 15

"You've what?" Dave said into the telephone the next morning.

"My frog," said the voice at the other end, "I've lost my frog." It was Stacy calling from the swim palace.

"When's the last time you had it?" Dave asked.

"Last night after we got back from the stadium, when we were talking to Speed Sloan."

"How soon does the diving begin?"

"Forty-five minutes," Stacy replied. "I guess it's silly to worry about a frog, but you know . . ."

"We'll do the best we can," promised Dave. He hung up the telephone and turned to Larry.

"What's wrong?" the other runner said.

"Stacy claims she's lost her frog," Dave explained. "And I've got a hunch where I might find it."

"Where are you going?" Dave asked.

"To see Speed Sloan."

The two quickly walked to the end of the hallway and stopped in front of Speed Sloan's room. They buzzed. Speed started to open the door. When he realized who wanted to come in he tried to shut it, but Dave shoved his way inside. "What do you guys want?" asked Speed.

"The frog," snapped Dave. "Where is it?"

"Oh that," Speed mumbled. "Stacy forgot it yesterday. I planned to return it to her."

"Sure you did," said Larry.

The metal frog sat on the dresser. Larry grabbed it. "I don't suppose you'd know anything about a tampered compass or a missing set of photographs," said Dave.

"I don't know what you're talking about," said Speed.

Dave wanted to punch him, but they had to take Stacy her frog. They left, but when they reached the bus depot, none of the buses were moving. "The marathon is being held today," explained one of the drivers.

Dave suddenly recalled that buses to the other side of town were being halted for three hours today. Traffic was being blocked because of the marathon, a long-distance running race that wound through the city streets. At Mexico City one of the swimmers had missed his event because he got stuck in traffic on the day of the marathon. "Well, that's that," said Larry. "No it isn't," Dave replied. "Come on."

They ran quickly back to his room. Dave rummaged through the closet. He found what he wanted in a bag—the pair of roller shoes. "Bus traffic may be stopped," he said, "but I can get through wearing these." He quickly laced the shoes onto his feet and grabbed Stacy's frog.

"The team orienteering starts in two hours," warned Larry. Team orienteering consisted of two men on a team. With Dave watching the compass and Larry pushing the pace, they felt they had a chance to finish with a high score.

"I'll be back," said Dave.

He moved quickly to the elevator. Soon Dave was skating swiftly along the streets. He reached the boulevard, where soldiers serving as traffic guards had traffic blocked for the marathoners, and darted quickly across.

"Hey, where are you going?" shouted one of the guards.

"Swim palace," said Dave, but did not stop.

"Come back here!" shouted another guard.

At that moment a captain of the guards arrived in a jeep and wanted to know the cause of the commotion. The two guards explained about the jaywalking roller skater.

"He can't get away with that," snorted the captain. "Which way was he going?"

"To the swim palace," answered the two guards.

The captain motioned for his two men to climb into the jeep. Then he turned to his driver, "Follow that roller skater!" With a clashing of gears, the jeep full of guards roared off in Dave Henderson's wake.

CHAPTER 16 Dave skated rapidly into the swim palace in time to see Stacy poised on top of the diving platform. "My gosh, I'm too late," he thought.

"Let's see your ticket," asked one of the guards.

Dave flashed him his press pass. He wondered for a minute how he could get Stacy's attention. He wanted her to know that he had her frog in hand.

He began to move toward the diving area. *Scrape, scrape,* went his roller skates against the tile of the pool. A number of Olympic officials sitting in the grandstand turned around and glared at him. "Shhhhh," they said.

81

At that moment Stacy hurled herself off the platform, turning and twisting and knifing smoothly into the water. Immediately the scoreboard lit up: 83.04 POINTS. A cheer rose from the crowd.

"Holy cow," thought Dave. "That's her best dive so far. And she did it without her good luck frog."

Stacy was climbing out of the water to the applause of the crowd. She toweled herself dry then turned and watched another diver go off the board.

Dave wondered if he should call to her and tell her he was here. But she had gotten her best score believing that the frog was lost. He decided to keep quiet.

"Dave, you brought my frog." It was too late, Stacy had spotted him.

"Good dive, Stacy," he said. She reached toward the stainless steel frog in his hand. He held it away from her. "You don't need the frog, Stacy. See how well you dove without it."

"Don't be silly," Stacy said, taking the frog from his hand. "If I dove that well without the frog, think of how well I can dive with it." She turned back toward the diving platform.

Dave shouted after her, "Stacy, you've got to break yourself of this frog habit."

One of the Olympic officials turned and glared at him again. "Young man, if you don't keep quiet, you're going out of here."

"Yes sir," said Dave.

He watched as another diver cut into the water.

Her dive hadn't been as good as Stacy's last one. Stacy had moved up from fourth to second place. Maybe there was a chance of her winning a gold medal.

It was Stacy's turn again. She set her frog near the side of the pool, then ascended to the top of the platform. The crowd hushed. Stacy launched herself into space. She twisted and turned, slicing into the water. An even more perfect dive than the last one.

But the computer didn't seem to think so. It scored her dive 77.39 points. The crowd groaned. That would cost Stacy dearly.

"She was robbed!" Dave shouted. "Kill the computer!"

Peter Powell, sitting in the group of Olympic officials, looked around and glared, trying to spot the person insulting his computer. Dave decided he better keep quiet.

The next dive was by an East German girl. It dropped Stacy to fourth, and another diver pushed her back to fifth. She had only one more dive left to try and make her gold medal.

Once more Stacy moved toward the diving platform. She placed her frog by the water's edge and started up the ladder.

Dave sat watching. Why should she dive so well without the frog and so badly with it. As Stacy reached the top of the platform, he stared at the steel frog sitting right above one of the sensor lenses.

Suddenly Dave stood up. "That's it," he realized. The frog was interfering with the sensor lens at that point. The steel would affect the magnetic circuits leading to the computer. Stacy could not get full credit for her dives.

"Wait!" he shouted and lunged forward.

But Dave had lunged forgetting he had roller skates on his feet. Suddenly he slid out of balance toward the diving platform.

Peter Powell stood up in the official's box. All at once he recognized the person with roller skates. "You!" he shouted.

Dave skidded on his skates toward the side of the pool and over its side. *Splash!* In the last second before he tumbled into the water he grabbed Stacy's metal frog.

"Seize that man!" shouted Powell to several guards near the grandstand.

Dave's head bobbed up in the water. He looked up at the top of the platform toward the diver. "Stacy," he shouted. "It's the frog. It's been shorting the computer."

Powell was red with rage. He pointed at Dave Henderson treading water in the diving area. "Stop him."

Three ushers stood by the side of the pool. They looked at each other, shrugged, then dove in.

"Oh my gosh," said Dave. Still holding the frog, he began to paddle toward the other end of the pool.

Two of the ushers began paddling after him. But the third usher was thrashing and struggling. "Help," he shouted. "I forgot I can't swim." One of the ushers turned back to save him.

As Dave swam the length of the pool, Powell stood on the edge. "I'll have you arrested," he raged. "I'll have you hung! I'll revoke your Olympic pass!"

Dave found himself at the shallow end of the pool. He started to climb out. At that moment the captain of the traffic guards burst into the pool, followed by his two men.

"There he is!" shouted the captain. "The jaywalker!"

"I surrender," said Dave, standing in water up to his neck.

"Get that man out of the pool!" shouted Powell.

The two guards reached down and grabbed Dave. They hauled him out of the pool by his armpits and pushed him away from the water's edge. The three ushers also climbed out of the pool. They all now stood next to the PED-72 computer, which scored all the swimming and diving events.

The captain of the guards snatched the frog from Dave's hands. "What's this?" he asked.

"A frog," Dave replied.

The captain grabbed Dave by the throat. "Confess," he said. "What is the meaning of this frog?"

"Quiet!" Peter Powell silenced everybody. He pointed toward the other end of the arena where Stacy stood on top of the diving platform. "The Olympics must go on. We'll deal with this fool later."

The Olympic chief began to walk back to his seat. The captain relaxed his grip on Dave's neck. While awaiting the dive, he placed the steel frog on top of the computer.

"No, wait—" Dave began. A glare from the captain silenced him. The two guards tightened their hold on his arms.

Stacy stood at the edge of the platform. The crowd quieted and turned its attention toward her. But the commotion had been too much for her. She started to dive, stopped, then suddenly lost her balance. She fell through the air feet first, thrashing with her arms. She landed in the water with a big *Buh-loomp*.

"Poor Stacy," Dave groaned.

Stacy surfaced. At that instant the computer scoreboard began flashing: 473,928.07 POINTS.

Powell was standing again. "What?"

The scoreboard continued to flash: STACY RANDOLPH'S TOTAL: 89,354,625,911.72 POINTS.

"That dive wasn't worth half a point," raged Powell. "Somebody's been tampering with my computer."

STACY RANDOLPH IS THE NEW OLYMPIC CHAMPION, announced the computer scoreboard.

"It's the frog," Dave tried to explain. "This time it shorted the entire computer."

Powell stood before Dave, his face a mask of hate. "This time you're really in trouble." The captain grabbed Dave again by the neck.

"Ggllmpghh," said Dave.

At that moment the scoreboard lit up in red, white, and blue—the American flag. The "Star Spangled Banner" began to play through the electronic sound system.

Automatically the captain and his two guards relaxed their hold on Dave, turned, and snapped to attention. They saluted smartly, as PED-72 began to spell out: OH, SAY CAN YOU SEE . . .

Dave suddenly found himself free. He began to skate as fast as he could toward the nearest exit.

"Come back here!" Powell screamed after him. "Don't you know it's unpatriotic to escape during the playing of the national anthem!"

CHAPTER 17

Dave skated as rapidly as he could toward the site of the orienteering meet. He glanced at his watch. He was late.

He could hear the shouts of the guards, who had come rushing out of the swim palace in pursuit of him. But he could make faster time through the crowded streets than they could.

Ten minutes later he skated into the clearing near the start of the orienteering meet. He slid to a halt and collapsed in the grass. Larry Spitzig ran up to him. "What happened?"

"Stacy won the gold medal," Dave replied.

"Did her frog do it?"

"Yes," replied Dave. "You might say that her frog did it."

At that minute the loudspeaker called their names. "It's our turn," said Larry. "Get those roller skates off."

Soon Dave and Larry stood at the line, map and compasses in hand. An orienteering official waited with them, holding a stopwatch. At that moment a long limousine appeared and screeched to a halt. Peter Powell jumped out at the same time that the captain and the two guards arrived in their jeep.

"There they are!" shouted Powell.

Larry turned to Dave. "What's happening?"

At that second the official dropped his hand. "Go," he said.

Dave started running toward the woods. "I'll explain later," he shouted over his shoulder. "Just go." Larry ran after him.

Powell turned to the captain. "Capture them!" he ordered.

The captain turned to the two guards. "Capture them!"

The two guards started to run toward the woods. They were stopped by the orienteering official. "You can't go there."

"Why not?" raged Powell.

"This is an Olympic event," explained the official. "Besides, they'd never find their way without map and compass."

"Then give them a map and compass," snorted

Powell. "Call them the Scandian team if you want. You let almost everybody else in your event."

The official shrugged and handed a map and compass to the two guards. They started off at a trot toward the woods.

Two more vans full of guards pulled up. Peter Powell waved the men past him. "To the woods. To the woods."

"But I—" protested the official.

Meanwhile, deep in the woods, Larry and Dave ran along a tree-lined path. Dave explained what had happened at the swim palace. "What do we do now?" asked Larry.

"I don't know," said Dave. "But I know I've got to get back to the track stadium in time to photograph the 1500-meter finals, or I'll lose my job."

They came into a clearing and saw a red flag. "Here's the first checkpoint," said Larry. They stopped and marked their cards. Dave took a quick reading with his compass and pointed off across a ridge.

They heard a crashing through the brush. "It's the traffic guards after me," said Dave.

"Maybe it's only another pair of orienteers," said Larry.

"I'm not stopping to find out," cried Dave. "Come on." They started off again at a run.

The second they disappeared the two guards appeared. They paused underneath the flag and looked in all directions. Then checking their map and compass, as had Larry and Dave, they ran off in pursuit again.

90

Ahead of them Larry and Dave ran along the bank of a stream. "What do we do?" asked Larry.

"Well, one thing we *don't* do is panic," said Dave. "Here's our next checkpoint."

They marked their cards, then started off in a new direction. They followed a path for several minutes, then started up the side of a hill. There was a crashing in the brush ahead of them. "Oh my gosh," said Dave and dove for the ground.

"What are you doing?" asked Larry.

"I'm panicking," said Dave. "Get down."

Two men rushed out of the brush and across the path. It was not guards but orienteers. One of the men spotted Dave and Larry lying on the ground. "Lost?" he said running past.

"No, just resting," said Dave.

The two orienteers disappeared. Larry and Dave rose from the ground.

At that moment a voice sounded behind them. "There they are." It was the two guards. "Stop!"

"Quick," shouted Dave. "Run."

The two ran off with the guards in pursuit. "We'll never lose them," said Larry. "They're using the same map we are."

"We could skip some of the checkpoints," suggested Dave.

"And break our Olympic oath?"

Dave grabbed Larry by the arm and pulled him into the bushes and down on the ground. "Forget about your Olympic oath," he whispered. "I'm going to miss the 1500 meters. *Sports Weekly* will never forgive me."

Within a few seconds the two guards came running through the brush. Dave and Larry lay still as they rushed past them. When the sound of their footsteps had faded, the two stood up.

"Do you think we're safe now?" asked Larry.

Before Dave could answer a voice came from behind him. "We've found them," it said. This time it was a different pair of guards.

Larry felt a strong pair of arms grip him from behind. "I think we're surrounded," he said.

"I think I've just lost my job," replied Dave.

CHAPTER 18 Dave and Larry were marched

back to the starting line where Peter Powell and the captain of the guards awaited them. "You are under arrest," announced the captain.

"Under arrest?" said Larry.

"You can't arrest us," said Dave. "What have we done?"

"Disrupted the Olympics," snapped Powell.

"Yes, you have disrupted the Olympics," echoed the captain. "The people of our country have waited long to host the Olympics. They will be unhappy at your disrupting it. Besides, you jaywalked."

"*Jayskated,*" Dave corrected him.

"Whatever you did, you're guilty," said the captain. "Jayskating is a serious crime."

"But that was only me," protested Dave. "Larry wasn't even there."

"Your friend is an accomplice," said the captain. "He probably will get off with only five to ten years."

"Five to ten years?" Larry moaned.

"At least," said the captain. "Away with the Americans!"

Olympic ushers marched the two American orienteers toward the waiting car.

"Captain," said one guard. "Your two men have not yet returned."

The captain looked in the direction of the woods. At that moment the two guards who first had set off in pursuit of Dave and Larry appeared. They sprinted toward the captain and saluted sharply. "We followed the course," announced one of the guards breathing heavily, "but we did not locate the two Americans."

"Fools!" shouted the captain. "They have already been found." He pointed toward the truck.

The two guards gazed toward Dave and Larry and wilted visibly.

"Away with the Americans," commanded the captain once again.

Before this could happen the orienteering official came running toward the group of men. "Captain. Captain. Are these two under your command?"

The captain turned toward him. "Have they done

anything wrong?" he asked. "If they have, they join the Americans in jail." The two guards looked worried.

"No, it is nothing like that," said the official. "Did they pass all the checkpoints on the orienteering course?"

The captain turned and glared at the two men. "Well?"

"We followed your orders, Captain," said one of the men. He handed a card to the captain who handed it to the official.

"What is happening?" grumbled Powell. "Why the delay?"

The official examined the card and nodded. Then he looked up at the captain. "Are you the coach of these two men?"

The captain looked puzzled. "Coach?" he said.

"What is this all about?" snapped Powell.

The orienteering official smiled. "These two guards just completed the course in the fastest time of the day. They are the Olympic champions."

"The Olympic *whats*?" roared Powell.

The orienteering official shook hands with the two men and then with the captain of the guards. "As their coach you should be very proud," said the official.

"Their coach?" babbled the captain.

"This is preposterous!" snarled Powell.

"Yes, their coach," the captain was talking to himself. "I will be promoted at least to Major."

"This can't happen!" shouted Powell.

"Maybe Colonel," the captain continued. "This is the first Olympic gold medal in Scandia's history."

"What about these two Americans?" asked Powell. "They've just been arrested."

The captain suddenly returned to reality. "Oh, they will be released of course. In honor of this happy event, all prisoners will be pardoned." The captain turned and placed his arms around the shoulders of his two guardsmen. A number of photographers began to swarm around taking pictures of him and the two new Olympic champions.

Dave and Larry stood forgotten. Dave glanced at his watch. "Come on," he whispered to his friend. "If we hurry we can get back to the Olympic stadium in time for the 1500 meters." Nearby a band started to play.

Powell turned in time to see them leaving. "Come back here!" he shouted.

But the captain turned and glared at Powell. "Silence," he shouted. "Can't you hear? They are playing the Scandian national anthem."

CHAPTER 19

Dave Henderson staggered into the press section of the Olympic stadium. He and Larry had run all the way from the orienteering course. Dave collapsed into a seat near where he had stored his camera gear. When he regained his breath, he asked Larry, "Did we make it in time?"

"They're almost ready to start the 1500 meters," said his friend.

With a sigh of relief, Dave reached for his telephoto camera. He sighted through it and saw Speed Sloan walking toward the starting line followed by Jim

Price, who had become Speed's new rabbit. Dr. Costello had convinced Price that he could share in Speed Sloan's glory in the finals by setting a fast, early pace for him. Price also wore Simba shoes. Dave wondered if the shoe salesman was paying both runners.

Even as Dave and Larry watched, Price stood beside Speed at the starting line. "You want the first lap in 55 seconds, right?" said the other American runner.

"Fifty-five-*point*-three," Speed corrected him. The strategy (as decided by Dr. Costello's computer) was to let Price set a too-fast pace over the first two laps of the nearly-four-lap race. Speed would lag behind by ten or twenty yards as his rivals burned themselves out trying to keep up with Price. Price would fade and so would the other runners. With one lap to go, Speed would burst ahead with a sprint finish that no one else would be able to match. Victory was assured.

Andrew Martin offered Sloan his hand. "Good luck, sport," said the African.

Sloan smiled thinly back at him. "Luck has nothing to do with it," he said.

The barefoot African shrugged his shoulders. An electronic voice called the eight 1500-meter finalists to the line at the head of the back straightaway. "Take your marks."

A hush fell over the huge stadium. The starting buzzer sounded. As planned, Jim Price burst sharply off the line to take the lead. Andrew Martin

98

started almost as fast. At the end of the first straightaway, the African slid in behind Price. The other runners bunched up quickly as they swept through the first curve. Speed moved effortlessly in the rear as the runners rushed down the next straightaway. Then they were around the second curve and past the 400-meter mark.

PED-72 immediately flashed the time for the first lap on both scoreboards. Price indeed had hit 55.3 seconds, with Andrew Martin a mere tenth of a second behind. The crowd gasped at the fast time.

Dave lowered his camera for a moment. "Can they hold that pace without cracking?"

"I don't think so," said Larry, shaking his head slowly. "Martin got pulled out too fast. He's right where Speed wants him."

As the runners moved down the back straightaway, Price still held the lead followed by Martin and three other runners. Then there was a gap of nearly ten yards, two other runners, and finally Speed Sloan.

Dave focused his camera again on the runners coming down the main straightaway. Swiftly he snapped the shutter. *Click. Click.* The runners went past beneath him and into the turn, then past the 800-meter mark at the head of the back straightaway.

Again PED-72 flashed the lap time of the leader: PRICE: 1:53.7. The pace had slowed somewhat, but was still faster than anyone had ever run on the way to 1500 meters before.

"Wow," said Dave.

"I'm worried that Martin won't last," commented Larry.

A gap of three yards separated Price and Martin from the next three runners from Australia, Russia, and Sweden. Then there was a still larger gap before Speed Sloan, who had moved into sixth place. The rest of the starters had fallen back.

"Sloan's coming on," shouted one of the reporters in the press section. "He's like a machine!"

"He *is* a machine," Larry corrected him.

Sloan passed the Swede halfway down the back straightaway and caught the Russian in the next turn. He didn't wait, but swept wide around him. Coming out of the turn and into the main straightaway he moved past the Australian into third place.

The fast pace had begun to tell on the two front runners. Price's form began to go. Andrew Martin moved around him into the lead. Dave clicked his camera quickly as the barefoot African rushed past the finish line. The buzzer sounded signaling one lap to go. Dave could see that Martin looked very, very tired. Would he fold?

Speed Sloan now had begun his sprint. He passed Price. At the end of lap three, 1200 meters, he had closed to within half a stride of the African. PED-72 flashed the time: 2:52.9, still a world record pace.

Going down the back straightaway Sloan moved wide to pass the last runner between him and his gold medal. His long legs stroked the track powerfully. His strong arms swung in rhythm with his legs.

It was the moment of truth. Eighty thousand people in the Olympic stadium stood and shouted as the two runners moved shoulder-to-shoulder down the straightaway. Sloan slowly began to inch ahead.

Up in the stands, Dave was so hypnotized by the battle for first, he almost forgot his job. His remote control camera had been set at the head of the final turn pointed directly at the approaching runners. "My camera," he suddenly shouted.

"Will it work?" asked Larry.

"I shifted the antenna on the radio transformer last night," Dave told him. "It should give a stronger signal." He pushed the button.

A rumbling noise came from high overhead. "What's that?" asked Larry.

Dave looked up. The giant roof of the domed stadium had begun to move. Blue sky showed above. "I'm not sure," moaned Dave, "but I think we're back in jail again."

Down on the track neither of the two lead runners realized the dome was opening above their heads. Sloan now had a half-stride lead, but Martin refused to die. They rushed toward the final turn. As they reached it, Sloan glanced to the left to see if he had room to cut in. At the same moment the African looked out toward Sloan. Their eyes met. And as they did a broad smile burst forth on the face of Andrew Martin.

The smile stunned Speed Sloan. Nobody smiles

during the final sprint of a 1500-meter run. Especially not the *Olympic* 1500 meters. According to the computer, no one should be near Speed Sloan at this point of the race. Suddenly the fight went out of Speed Sloan. Andrew Martin swept past him on the inside and back into the lead.

Vummm! sounded a large tube atop the scoreboard. Then *Vummm! Vummm! Vummm!* Four golden trails of smoke streaked into the sky above the now open stadium. *Kuh-bammm!!* An explosion of lights red, yellow, green, and blue burst overhead. Then another explosion of light. And two more.

"What's happening now?" Larry asked Dave up in the stands.

"It's the fireworks," said Dave. Even as he spoke a half-dozen more skyrockets roared up into the sky. "But they weren't supposed to go off until the closing ceremony tomorrow."

Suddenly Larry noticed the electronic radio control in Dave's hand. Dave said he had made its signal stronger. "Oh no," said Larry.

"That's right," nodded Dave. "I think we've wounded PED-72."

And at that moment Andrew Martin crossed the finish line his arms spread in a victory salute, Speed Sloan staggered off the track to collapse in the infield, two thousand doves suddenly flew into the air, skyrockets continued to pop, music sounded, and PED-72 flashed on the scoreboards one final message: GOODBYE UNTIL THE NEXT OLYMPICS.

CHAPTER 20 Dave Henderson sat at a desk in the offices of *Sports Weekly* magazine a week later and admired the cover of its latest issue. The photograph had been taken by him—or rather, his remote control camera.

It showed Andrew Martin and Speed Sloan looking at each other going into the final turn of the Olympic 1500-meter run. Martin had a big grin on his face, while Sloan's face showed fear. It was the moment at which the race had been won and lost. He had captured it on film. The managing editor offered him a raise after seeing that shot and reading the story of his exploits as an orienteer.

Andrew Martin had won an Olympic gold medal, but had missed breaking the world record. When PED-72 went crazy—because of Dave's radio signal to his robot camera—the timing devices also failed. The officials, meanwhile, had so trusted the computer that none had started a stopwatch. Nobody knew Martin's winning time. The African said he didn't care. He announced after his victory that he was retiring from track to become an orienteer. "It seems like more fun."

Peter Powell had resigned from the Olympic committee in disgrace, because of the computer failure. Only Dave knew, however, that it had been Powell himself who had sneaked into Larry's room. He had stolen the photographs (to protect Speed) and had tampered with the compass.

Dave learned this very easily. He asked the computer. PED-72 had seen, and PED-72 had told. Computers aren't bad by themselves; it's the people who program them.

Dr. Costello had returned to his laboratory. "No more human beings," the scientist announced. "I'm going back to working with field mice. They're much more predictable." After his defeat, Speed Sloan had vanished. And all over the world, track runners had begun to discard their spiked shoes to run barefoot. Sales of Simba shoes had almost stopped.

Dave laid down the copy of the magazine and

reached for the telephone. He dialed Stacy Randolph's number. Stacy kept her gold medal in platform diving. Everyone agreed she would have won anyway if the computer had scored her early dives properly.

"Good news, Stacy," Dave said when the girl answered. "The managing editor told me we may name you our 'Sportsman of the Year.' "

"But I'm not a man," protested the voice on the other end. "Besides, I've got my frog. I don't need a Greek vase."

"Do you need a date for dinner tomorrow night?" Dave asked.

"I might need that," Stacy agreed.

After Dave finished talking to Stacy, he made one more telephone call. He dialed Larry Spitzig.

"Larry, I've got very important news," Dave announced. "We've just got a press release from the Olympic committee."

"Nothing bad, I hope," said Larry.

"No, it's good," explained Dave. "They're adding a new sport to the Olympic Games four years from now. Guess what it is?"

"Tell me," asked Larry.

"Roller skating," said Dave. Larry was still laughing when he hung up the telephone.

ABOUT THE AUTHOR Hal Higdon's particular fields of interest—sports and humor—both date from an early age. He was an avid collector of comic books, and while still in his teens, he began to draw his own cartoons. After a short career as a magazine editor, he became a free-lance writer. His articles have appeared in such publications as *Sports Illustrated, The New York Times Magazine,* and *Playboy. The Horse That Played Center Field,* also a Pacesetter, was published in 1969.

Mr. Higdon's involvement with sports is active as well as literary. All along, he says, "I've sort of pursued two careers: one as a writer and one as a long-distance runner." In addition to winning several National A.A.U. championships, he was the first American to finish in the Boston Marathon in 1964. Like Dave Henderson, he wanted very much to make the Olympic team; only an injury stopped him.

To this day, he continues to run along the shores of Lake Michigan where he lives with his wife and three children.